The
HELEN OXENBURY
Nursery Rhyme Book

The HELEN OXENBURY Nursery Rhyme Book

Rhymes chosen by Brian Alderson

Young Lions

An Imprint of HarperCollinsPublishers

First published in Great Britain by William Heinemann Ltd 1986
First published in Young Lions 1990
Second impression 1991

Young Lions is an imprint of the Children's Division,
part of HarperCollins Publishers Limited,
77-85 Fulham Palace Road, Hammersmith,
London W6 8JB

Printed and bound by HarperCollins Hong Kong

Girls and boys, come out to play,
The moon doth shine as bright as day;
Leave your supper, and leave your sleep,
And come with your playfellows into the street.
Come with a whoop, come with a call,
Come with a good will or not at all.
Up the ladder and down the wall,
A halfpenny roll will serve us all.
You find milk and I'll find flour,
And we'll have a pudding in half an hour.

A, B, C, tumble down D,
The cat's in the cupboard and can't see me.

Apple-pie, pudding and pancake,
All begins with an A.

1, 2, 3, 4, 5!
I caught a hare alive;
6, 7, 8, 9, 10!
I let her go again.

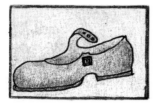

One, two,
Buckle my shoe;

Three, four,
Shut the door;

Five, six,
Pick up sticks;

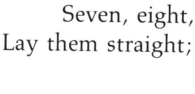

Seven, eight,
Lay them straight;

Nine, ten,
A good fat hen;

Eleven, twelve,
Who will delve;

Thirteen, fourteen,
Maids a-courting;

Fifteen, sixteen,
Maids a-kissing;

Seventeen, eighteen,
Maids a-waiting;

Nineteen, twenty,
My stomach's empty.

When Jacky's a very good boy,
    He shall have cakes and custard;
When he does nothing but cry,
    He shall have nothing but mustard.

There was an old woman who lived in a shoe,
She had so many children she didn't know what to do;
She gave them some broth without any bread,
She whipped them all well and put them to bed.

Little Tommy Tittlemouse
Lived in a little house;

He caught fishes
In other men's ditches.

Solomon Grundy,
Born on a Monday,

Christened on Tuesday,

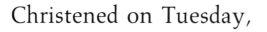

Married on Wednesday,

Took ill on Thursday,

Worse on Friday,

Died on Saturday,

Buried on Sunday;

This is the end
Of Solomon Grundy.

Sing a song of sixpence,
   A pocket full of rye;
Four and twenty blackbirds
   Baked in a pie;

When the pie was opened
   The birds began to sing;
Wasn't that a dainty dish
   To set before the king?

The king was in his counting house
   Counting out his money;
The queen was in the parlour
   Eating bread and honey;

The maid was in the garden
   Hanging out the clothes,
There came a little blackbird,
   And snapped off her nose.

Jenny was so mad,
   She didn't know what to do;
She put her finger in her ear,
   And cracked it right in two.

Hey! diddle, diddle,
The cat and the fiddle,
The cow jumped over the moon;
The little dog laughed
To see the sport,
While the dish ran after the spoon.

Three blind mice, see how they run!
They all ran after the farmer's wife,
Who cut off their tails with the carving-knife,
Did ever you see such fools in your life?
                        Three blind mice.

Ding, dong, bell,
Pussy's in the well!
Who put her in?—
Little Tommy Lin.
Who pulled her out?—
Dog with long snout.
What a naughty boy was that
To drown poor pussy-cat,
Who never did any harm,
But kill'd the mice in his father's barn.

Tweedle-dum and Tweedle-dee
   Resolved to have a battle,
For Tweedle-dum said Tweedle-dee
   Had spoiled his nice new rattle.
Just then flew by a monstrous crow,
   As big as a tar barrel,
Which frightened both the heroes so,
   They quite forgot their quarrel.

When good king Arthur ruled this land,
  He was a goodly king;
He stole three pecks of barley-meal,
  To make a bag-pudding.

A bag-pudding the king did make,
  And stuff'd it well with plums;
And in it put great lumps of fat,
  As big as my two thumbs.

The king and queen did eat thereof,
  And noblemen beside;
And what they could not eat that night,
  The queen next morning fried.

Peter White will ne'er go right.
  Would you know the reason why?
He follows his nose where'er he goes,
  And that stands all awry.

Elsie Marley is grown so fine,
She won't get up to serve the swine,
But lies in bed till eight or nine,
And surely she does take her time.

And do you ken Elsie Marley, honey?
The wife who sells the barley, honey;
She won't get up to serve her swine,
And do you ken Elsie Marley, honey?

Little girl, little girl, where have you been?
Gathering roses to give to the queen.
Little girl, little girl, what gave she you?
She gave me a diamond as big as my shoe.

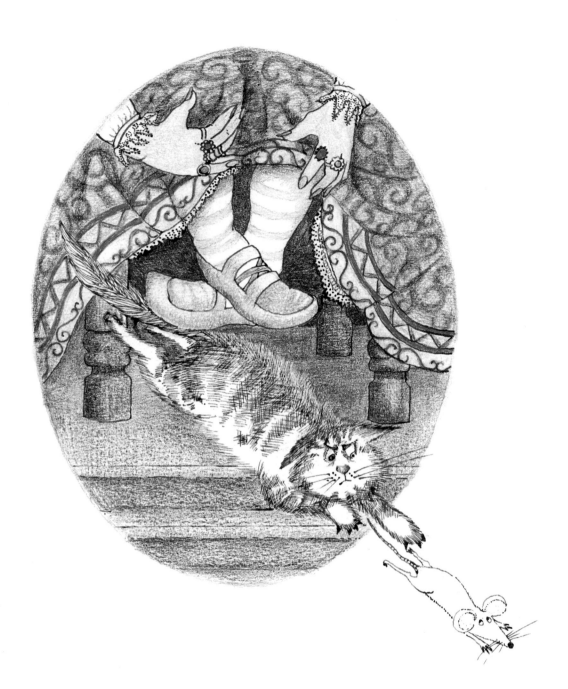

Pussy-cat, pussy-cat, where have you been?
I've been up to London to look at the queen.
Pussy-cat, pussy-cat, what did you there?
I frightened a little mouse under the chair.

The lion and the unicorn
    Were fighting for the crown;
The lion beat the unicorn
    All round the town.
Some gave them white bread,
    And some gave them brown;
Some gave them plum-cake,
    And sent them out of town.

Hector Protector was dressed all in green;
Hector Protector was sent to the Queen.
The Queen did not like him,
Nor more did the King:
So Hector Protector was sent back again.

Curly locks, curly locks, wilt thou be mine?
Thou shalt not wash dishes, nor yet feed the swine;
But sit on a cushion and sew a fine seam,
And feed upon strawberries, sugar, and cream.

Baa, baa, black sheep,
    Have you any wool?
Yes, marry, have I,
    Three bags full:

One for my master,
    And one for my dame,
But none for the little boy
    Who cries in the lane.

Rock-a-bye baby, thy cradle is green;
Father's a nobleman, mother's a queen;
And Betty's a lady, and wears a gold ring;
And Johnny's a drummer, and drums for the king.

I had a little husband,
　　No bigger than my thumb,
I put him in a pint pot,
　　And there I bid him drum.

I bought a little horse,
　　That galloped up and down;
I bridled him, and saddled him,
　　And sent him out of town.

I gave him some garters,
　　To garter up his hose,
And a little handkerchief,
　　To wipe his pretty nose.

As I was going up Pippen-hill,
    Pippen-hill was dirty,
There I met a pretty miss,
    And she dropped me a curtsey.

Little miss, pretty miss,
    Blessings light upon you!
If I had half-a-crown a day,
    I'd spend it all upon you.

Master I have, and I am his man,
    Gallop a dreary dun;
Master I have, and I am his man,
And I'll get a wife as fast as I can;
With a heighly gaily gamberaily,
    Higgledy piggledy, niggledy, niggledy,
    Gallop a dreary dun.

I had a young man,
He was double-jointed,
When I kissed him,
He was disappointed.

When he died
I had another one,
God bless his little heart,
I found a better one.

If you sneeze on Monday, you sneeze for danger;
Sneeze on a Tuesday, kiss a stranger;
Sneeze on a Wednesday, sneeze for a letter;
Sneeze on a Thursday, something better;
Sneeze on a Friday, sneeze for sorrow;
Sneeze on a Saturday, see your sweetheart tomorrow.

See this pretty little girl of mine,
She brought me a penny and a bottle of wine.
A bottle of wine and a penny too,
See what my little girl can do.

The fair maid who, the first of May,
Goes to the fields at break of day,
And washes in dew from the hawthorn tree,
Will ever after handsome be.

On Saturday night
Shall be all my care,
To powder my locks
And curl my hair.

On Sunday morning
My love will come in,
When he will marry me
With a gold ring.

Needles and pins, needles and pins,
When a man marries his trouble begins.

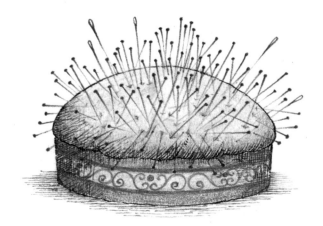

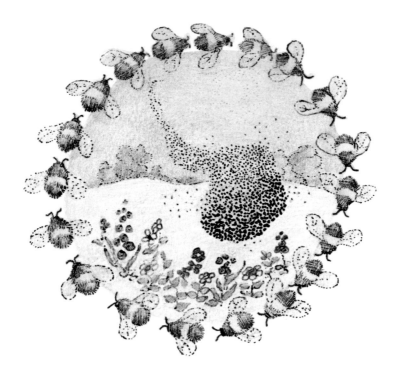

A swarm of bees in May
Is worth a load of hay;

A swarm of bees in June
Is worth a silver spoon;

A swarm of bees in July
Is not worth a fly.

There was a piper, he'd a cow;
    And he'd no hay to give her;
He took his pipes and played a tune,
    Consider, old cow, consider!

The cow considered very well,
    For she gave the piper a penny,
That he might play the tune again,
    Of corn rigs are bonnie!

What are little boys made of, made of,
What are little boys made of?
Snaps and snails and puppy-dogs' tails;
And that's what little boys are made of, made of.

What are little girls made of, made of,
What are little girls made of?
Sugar and spice, and all that's nice;
And that's what little girls are made of, made of.

Don't Care didn't care,
Don't Care was wild,
Don't Care stole plum and pear
Like any beggar's child.

Don't Care was made to care,
Don't Care was hung.
Don't Care was put in a pot
And boiled till he was done.

Little Tom Tucker
Sings for his supper;
What shall he eat?
White bread and butter.
How shall he cut it
Without e'er a knife?
How will he be married
Without e'er a wife?

Twelve huntsmen with horns and hounds,
Hunting over other men's grounds.

Eleven ships sailing o'er the main,
Some bound for France and some for Spain:
I wish them all safe home again:

Ten comets in the sky,
Some low and some high;

Nine peacocks in the air,
I wonder how they all come there,
I do not know, and do not care;

Eight joiners in joiner's hall,
Working with the tools and all;

Seven lobsters in a dish,
As fresh as any heart could wish;

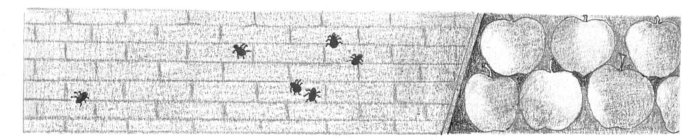

Six beetles against the wall,
Close by an old woman's apple stall;

Five puppies of our dog Ball,
Who daily for their breakfast call;

Four horses stuck in a bog;

Three monkeys tied to a clog;

Two pudding-ends would choke a dog;

With a gaping, wide-mouthed, waddling frog.

There was an old woman sat spinning,
And that's the first beginning;
    She had a calf,
    And that's half,
She took it by the tail,
And threw it over the wall,
And that's all.

Baby and I
   Were baked in a pie,
The gravy was wonderful hot;
   We had nothing to pay
   To the baker that day,
And so we crept out of the pot.

I am a little beggar girl,
My mother she is dead,
My father is a drunkard
And won't give me no bread.
I look out of the window
To hear the organ play—
God bless my dear mother,
She's gone far away.

Little Polly Flinders
Sat among the cinders
Warming her pretty little toes.
Her mother came and caught her
And whipped her little daughter
For spoiling of her nice new clothes.

Jack Sprat could eat no fat,
　　His wife could eat no lean;
And so, betwixt them both, you see,
　　They licked the platter clean.

Eaper Weaper, chimbley sweeper,
Had a wife but couldn't keep her;
Had anovver, didn't love her,
Up the chimbley he did shove her.

Last night and the night before
Twenty-five robbers knocked at the door.
Johnny got up to let them in
And hit them on the head with a rolling pin.

Desperate Dan
The dirty old man
Washed his face
In a frying-pan;
Combed his hair
With the leg of a chair;
Desperate Dan
The dirty old man.

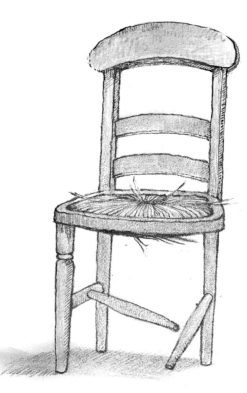

House to let,
Rent to pay,
Knock at the door
And run away.

Up and down Pie Street,
    The windows made of glass,
Call at Number Thirty-three,
    You'll see a pretty lass.

Her name is Annie Robinson,
    Catch her if you can,
She married Charlie Anderson,
    Before he was a man.

Bread and dripping all the week,
    Pig's head on Sunday,
Half a crown on Saturday night,
    A farthing left for Monday.

She only bought a bonnet-box,
    He only bought a ladle,
So when the little baby came
    It hadn't got no cradle.

Barber, barber, shave a pig,
How many hairs will make a wig?
"Four and twenty, that's enough,"
Give the barber a pinch of snuff.

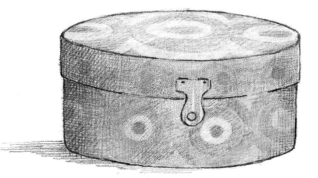

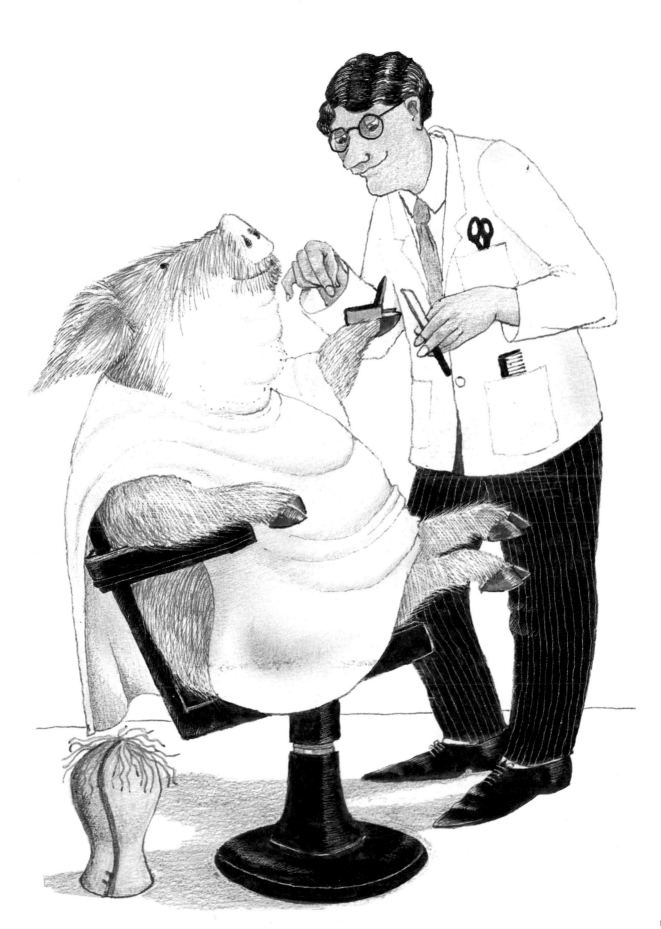

Policeman, policeman, don't take me!
Take that man behind that tree!
I stole brass, he stole gold.
Policeman, policeman, don't take hold!

Who comes here?
  A grenadier.
What do you want?
  A pot of beer.
Where's your money?
  I've forgot.
Then get you gone
  You drunken sot!

Trip upon trenchers, and dance upon dishes,
My mother sent me for some barm, some barm;

She bid me tread lightly, and come again quickly,
For fear the young men should do me some harm.

Yet didn't you see, yet didn't you see,
What naughty tricks they put upon me:

They broke my pitcher,
    And spilt the water,
And huffed my mother,
    And chid her daughter,

And kissed my sister instead of me.

Rosemary green,
And lavender blue,
Thyme and sweet marjoram,
Hyssop and rue.

Gray goose and gander,
   Waft your wings together,
And carry the good king's daughter
   Over the one strand river.

A man of words and not of deeds,
Is like a garden full of weeds;
And when the weeds begin to grow,
It's like a garden full of snow;
And when the snow begins to fall,
It's like a bird upon the wall;
And when the bird away does fly,
It's like an eagle in the sky;
And when the sky begins to roar,
It's like a lion at the door;
And when the door begins to crack,
It's like a stick across your back;
And when your back begins to smart,
It's like a penknife in your heart;
And when your heart begins to bleed,
You're dead, and dead and dead indeed!

INDEX OF FIRST LINES